AUBURN-PLACER
4665840

Fat Chance Thanksgiving

WRITTEN BY
Patricia Lakin

ILLUSTRATED BY
Stacey Schuett

Albert Whitman & Company
Morton Grove, Illinois

Library of Congress Cataloging-in-Publication Data

Lakin, Patricia.

Fat chance Thanksgiving / by Patricia Lakin; illustrated by Stacey Schuett

p. cm.

Summary: When their apartment burns down and they move to a much smaller place, Mama tells Carla they can't have Thanksgiving, but Carla thinks about all the hardships the Pilgrims faced and figures out a way.

ISBN 0-8075-2288-0 (hardcover)

[1. Thanksgiving Day — Fiction. 2. Neighbors — Fiction.

3. Apartment houses — Fiction. 4. New York (N.Y.) — Fiction.] I. Schuett, Stacey, ill. II. Title.

PZ7.L1586 Fat 2001 [E] — dc21 2001000803

Published in 2001 by Albert Whitman & Company, 6340 Oakton Street, Morton Grove, Illinois 60053-2723.

Published simultaneously in Canada by General Publishing, Limited, Toronto.

Printed in the United States of America.

10 9 8 7 6 5 4 3 2 1

The paintings are rendered in acrylic and gouache on Arches watercolor paper.

The text typeface is Allise.

The design is by Scott Piehl.

For more information about Albert Whitman & Company, visit our web site at www.albertwhitman.com

For Karen Brothers . . . social worker extraordinaire. — P. L.

For my mother. — S. S.

THE FIRE ATE EVERYTHING when it swept through Carla and Mama's apartment building.

All Carla had left was her book, *A Pilgrim Thanksgiving*.

"You can take it to the hotel the Red Cross found for us," Mama told her.

That was one year ago.

Each night, Carla curled up on her bed in the dark, cramped hotel room and read her book. Whenever she got to the last page, she pretended she was the smiling Pilgrim girl in the brown dress, sitting at the feast table surrounded by family and friends.

It was almost Thanksgiving when Mama got the news.

"We've got our own place!" she told Carla. "Our name finally came up on the housing list. We can move into our new apartment tomorrow."

"At last!" said Carla as she hugged Mama and her book.

The next morning, they stood on the subway platform.

"You're awfully quiet," said Mama.

"We're Pilgrims," said Carla, "sailing to the New World."

Mama chuckled. "We're sailing to the Upper West Side of Manhattan."

But Carla wasn't listening. She was boarding the *Mayflower.* It didn't matter that it looked just like the Seventh Avenue Subway.

Carla swayed to and fro. She held her head high as the ship sailed through the darkness.

After an hour's ride, Carla and Mama climbed up the subway stairs and into the morning light.

Soon they put their suitcases down in the lobby of a red brick building.

"Our new home," said Mama.

"Our Plymouth Rock," said Carla.

"Watch it!" a boy shouted as he barreled past them.

Carla unlocked the door marked 5-E. She and Mama stood and hugged in the beam of sunlight that shone through their window.

"Beautiful." Mama stroked the flowered sofa.

"Finally!" said Carla. "We're in our new land just like the Pilgrims! Now we can have a Thanksgiving feast, too."

"Fat chance," said Mama as she unpacked.

"Why? Thanksgiving's two whole weeks away."

"Look at our stove and refrigerator . . . tiny!"

"The Pilgrims didn't have any of those things."

"It's tough for us now," said Mama. "We don't have much money and all our friends are far away."

"It was tough for the Pilgrims, too . . . crossing that ocean and then learning to farm. But they had a BIG feast," said Carla.

Mama stroked Carla's hair. "Let's be thankful for what we do have and not wish for the impossible."

On Monday, Mama brought Carla to her new school. The boy from the lobby was in Carla's class. His name was Julio. The class made corn muffins. Everyone was asked about Thanksgiving plans.

"None," said Julio.

"We're having a big feast at our house," said Carla.

"You told a whopper!" said Julio.

"We are *so* having a big feast!" Carla snapped.

"Where?" he said. "We've all got teeny apartments."

G H K L M

After school, Carla pleaded once more for a big feast.

Mama gave her usual answer: "Fat chance."

Carla sank down on her bed, opened her book, and stared at her favorite picture. If only she could really be that Pilgrim girl. She'd know everybody. She could say, "Let's meet at the Common House to plan a huge feast."

Carla knew Julio was right. The apartments *were* small. But the Pilgrim houses were small, too. Wait— couldn't the lobby be a kind of meeting place, just like the Pilgrims' Common House?

She raced down the hall and told Julio her plan. "I need your help," she said.

"All I have to do is knock on doors and ask people if they want to share a little bit of food?"

Carla nodded.

"I guess so," Julio finally said. "But first we've got to ask Mr. Lewis. He runs the building."

Mr. Lewis kept scratching his chin. "People here tend not to mix. How are you going to get them together for a party?"

"Let her try," Julio pleaded.

"Well," he said, "if ten people agree, I'll let you do it."

"Done!" said Julio. He grabbed Carla by the hand and they tore downstairs.

The first two people said no before Julio finished talking. The third was a nice old man with a bushy gray beard. "My wife and I might have come," he said, "but we're going to a friend's house."

Carla sighed as they walked down to the next floor. Maybe Mr. Lewis was right.

"Yes?" a lady peeked out from behind 6-A. She held a sleeping baby. "I don't know anyone in the building," she said softly. "Maybe I'll attend next year."

"But Mama and I don't know anyone either, Mrs. Li," said Carla.

"Well, maybe I'll bring something. But I won't stay."

A dog barked when they knocked on the next door.

"Hi, Mrs. Scully," Julio greeted the lady with the fluffy hair. He told her about the Thanksgiving feast.

"Mickie, you hear that?" she told her dog. "But I can't make a lot of food."

"Just bring one dish," Carla told her. "We'll all share."

"Then I'll bring two dishes," she said. "Irish stew for us and dog biscuits for Mickie!"

They knocked on the door across the hall. Reggae music seeped out when a man and a little boy opened their door. "Yes?" the man asked.

"We wanted to ask you to our Thanksgiving feast," said Carla. "Everyone brings a dish. It starts at noon in the lobby."

"We can make it!" He extended his hand. "I'm Jeremiah. So is he," the man said as he patted his son's shoulders. "I'll make my mom's roti bread."

"I count six yeses," Carla said. "Mama, me, you, Mrs. Scully, and the two Jeremiahs. We need four more."

"My papi will come. He makes great arroz con pollo," said Julio. "And count Mrs. Li and her baby as two yeses."

"But that's only nine people."

"Then count Mickie," said Julio.

"The dog?" Carla laughed. "Why not!"

"A deal's a deal," said Mr. Lewis when he heard their news. "Can I come, even if I can't cook?" He snapped his fingers. "But I can share my folding tables."

"Yes!" Carla jumped up and down.

That whole week, Carla and Julio made place mats and decorations. And more people told Carla that they'd come, too.

On Thanksgiving morning, Carla ran to the lobby. Mr. Lewis had set up one long feast table. Mama helped Carla, Julio, and his papi put up the decorations. By noon, people started bringing their chairs and covered dishes.

Mama made friends with Mickie first.

Julio took the plate from Mrs. Li. "Chocolate-chip cookies!" he cheered. Mrs. Li smiled and began helping Mama set out the place mats.

There was salsa and chips, Mama's bread pudding, fried okra, arroz con pollo made by Julio's papi, Jeremiah's roti bread, Mrs. Scully's Irish stew, Carla and Julio's corn muffins, black-eyed peas, lasagna, sweet potato pie, turkey, stuffing, apple cider, dog biscuits, and a mountain of chocolate-chip cookies.

Papi brought candles and his guitar. Jeremiah brought his drums.

When everyone was seated, Mr. Lewis held up his cup. "Let's say what we're all thankful for," he suggested. "I know I'm glad to see this lobby put to good use."

Julio went next. "And I'm glad about the chocolate-chip cookies!" he said. "Thanks, Mrs. Li. They're the best."

"I'm grateful for our new home and new neighbors," said Mama. "But mostly, I'm thankful for my daughter Carla and her Fat Chance Thanksgiving!"

Carla smiled at Mama and all of the friends gathered around the wonderful feast table. Their faces glowed in the candlelight. This picture wasn't like the one in *A Pilgrim Thanksgiving*.

For Carla, this picture was much, much better.